Collins…and the letter

This novel about the mysterious letter Collins finds on the street takes the reader on a journey through a labyrinth of coincidences from Cork City over to Perugia, and from there down to Rome. The letter arouses in Collins all sorts of speculations and fantasies. Who is Mary Murphy? How come she gets a letter from Rome? What's Finbar Barry doing in Rome? What is their relationship? While Collins goes from pub to pub talking about lost letters, trying to unravel the mystery, we learn about why Finbar went to Perugia and finally to Rome. We are given an insight to his life there with Silke up to when, years later, he meets a group of lads from Cork. From them he learns about some writer in Cork, and decides to write to his old girlfriend Mary. Collins thinks it's stuff for a novel, but first he must travel to Rome to meet Barry.

Books by Mike Crowley

Poems and Limericks
What Colette didn't know
Pledged in Green
Wild thoughts trapped in Verse
Collins…and the letter
Tinged Ideas

Mike Crowley was born in Cork City. He lives in Frankfurt.

Thanks to Gertrude Gebauer for checking the manuscript.

Mike Crowley

Collins…and the letter

ISBN: 978-1-913275-78-5

This book was published in cooperation with Choice Publishing, Drogheda, Co. Louth, Republic of Ireland.
www.choicepublishing.ie

Cast a cold eye
on life, on death.
Horseman, pass by!
(WB Yeats)

Chapter One

Post for Mary Murphy

It's me all right.

Still in his pyjamas, and a dressing-gown wrapped round him, he was standing in front of the mirror in the bathroom brushing his teeth. About an hour earlier, when the alarm clock pulled him out of his sleep, he was right in the middle of a dream; something about a letter. He stretched out his arm and turned off the alarm. Christ's sake, he cursed, have I nothing more entertaining to think about in my sleep?

On his way home the night before he happened to find a letter on the pavement. At first he wanted to ignore it and walk on. But then, on second thoughts, he bent down, picked it up and read the address. Not far from here, he said to himself, putting the letter into his coat pocket. I can drop it into the letter-box in the morning on my way to the library. He gets out of bed, switches on the light in the hall, where he slips into a pair of sandals, and goes out to the letter-box to collect the morning paper. Bleak, he mutters, glancing at the sky. By the looks of it, it must have rained a lot in the night. The small birds were chattering in the nearby hedges. Ah, spring, he muses, spring at last, though the weather isn't playing up to it. He pulls the newspaper from the letter-box, goes in and closes the door. Lovers still lying in the hay, he muses, having a rattle before getting ready for the day, and he smiles, thinking about the times when an odd girlfriend used to stay overnight.

Wire on fire, said Mcguire,
Whishkey and fla, said Mcgrath.
We'll settle for gin, said O'Flynn.

He chuckles. Ar eiri dom ar maiden/ when I get up in the morning, he croons, taking the newspaper into the kitchen. There he finds the letter on the table. Oh, the letter, he moans, picking it up. Mary Murphy, he reads, and on the reverse of the envelope: Finbar Barry, fermoinposta, Via Silvestro, Roma. Private address, he thinks, sounds like a Cork man, friend of hers living in Rome. Wonder what's he doing there? Well, first things first, he says to himself, putting the letter back on the table, and goes about preparing breakfast. He believes in having a good breakfast, and agrees fully with the saying: Morning like a king, midday like a prince, and evening like a beggar. However, he chuckles, who would have anything against a sumptuous evening meal? Haha! He pours water into the water-boiler, and spoons coffee into the filter. From the fridge he takes two eggs and a tube of mustard. He cracks the eggs onto the sizzling chopped onion and cuts two slices of bread. The boiler makes a kind of grunt, announcing that the water is boiled. He scolds the coffee pot, fixes the filter and pours water over the coffee. He turns off the stove and puts a mug on the table. Then he tosses the fry onto a plate, adds a generous sprinkling of salt and pepper and a squirt of mustard. He puts the mustard back into the fridge, puts the fry on the table, and pours coffee. He doesn't take milk in his coffee and, as he puts it himself, he relishes the wild, almost toxic flavour of black coffee. Just as he sits down to the table, a familiar tapping on the window makes him turn and look. As if we hadn't enough rain already, he moans, taking the fork and knife and digging into his fry. Munching his food, his eyes can't help reminding him of the letter beside him on the table. Poor Mary Murphy, he thinks, by now she must have ransacked the house searching for the letter.

> *I know damn well I put it into my bag. Pickpockets? And bloody hell I haven't even read it. Hope Finbar hasn't any indecent remarks in it. And now I'm going to have to write him that I got his letter, but unfortunately couldn't read it because I lost it. Would Finbar believe that?*

He drinks down his coffee and pours another mug. And then, just like out of the blues, he thinks:Now why in the bloody hell couldn't I have thought about that last night? Poor Mrs. Murphy worrying about where she put the letter, and all I had to do was to give her a ring.

> *Sorry to bother you so late, but I'm sure you'll be pleased to hear that I found your letter.*
> *You did? She screams. Ah, I tell you, sir, I've been searching for it since I came home yesterday evening and couldn't find it.*
> *I'm sure you have. Well, I'll drop it in to you in the morning on my way to the library.*
> *Oh, sir, that's awfully kind of you.*

Bullshit, he thinks, too late for that now, and a bit early to phone her yet.

So, that was a good start for the day, he tells himself, emptying his mug. He gets up from the table, rolls up his shirtsleeves, and does the wash up. That done, he sits down again and busies himself with the newspaper. After glancing through the headlines, he turns to the Deaths. Just like he heard it the previous day: South Chapel at

11 o'clock. In the bedroom after a shave and a shower, he considers wearing black, but right away rejects the idea. A black tie will do the job all right. Outside the dark clouds disperse and a watery beam of sunshine enters the room. Oh, looks like it's stopped raining, he says to himself, time to get going. Can never trust these weather-men, he muses, "When the cock crows on the dunghill, the weather will change or remain as it is." What bullshit! When he's dressed, he pulls on his overcoat, takes the letter from the table, and puts it into his pocket. He gets the books for the library and, standing in the hallway considers, whether to take an umbrella or not. Maybe come in handy, he thinks, grabbing the umbrella, and leaving the house he hums "three coins in the fountain," Watching his step not to slip on the wet ground, lalala.

Never been to Rome. Oh yes, "Some-where in the heart of Rome." Rome wasn't built in a day. Passing his local at the bottom of the hill, where he had a few jars the evening before, a sour stink of beer met his nose. Glad I didn't mention the letter, he thinks. Crossing Patrick's bridge a raw breeze mingled with drops of rain blowing up from the docks, ruffled the surface of the river. He hangs the umbrella on one arm, unfastens the upper button of his coat and tucks the two books inside it. Must be careful not to get them wet, he says to himself. I might have left you at home, he says to the umbrella, but who knows, you might come in handy yet.

Wonder what Mary Murphy‘s like? What kind of bird could she be? Friend in Rome. Now, supposing instead of I dropping the letter into the letter-box, I just rang her bell?

> *Sorry to bother you, Mrs. Murphy, I've just moved in, and to my surprise a letter for you somehow landed in my letter-box.*
> *How come, I wonder?*
> *No idea, so I thought I'd hand it to you.*
> *Oh, how awfully nice of you, sir. You shouldn't have gone to all that trouble.*
> *No trouble at all, Mrs. Murphy.*
> *From Rome, she mutters, after taking the letter and reading the sender's address.*
> *Yes, I saw that myself, a friend in Rome.*
> *Oh, gosh, sir, I was never in Rome, and friends I haven't got there either.*

Well, Mrs. Murphy, the letter is for you, and it's from Rome.

Mary Murphy looks at the letter as if searching her memory.

Now, that I think about it, she says, it's a long time ago. I think I did know some fellow who went to Italy, maybe Rome.

'Twill probably come clear to you when you read the letter, Mrs. Murphy.

Let's hope so, sir, and thanks for your trouble.

Hold on, he says to himself, recovering from his monologue, and realizing the house he was looking for was just a few houses away. Here we are. So, let's see. O'Shea Grant Murray no Murphy. Well, let's try the door-bells. Nothing doing, no Murphy. Wondering he puts the letter back into his pocket, and goes off to the library.

Just returning the books, he says to the lady at the desk. Won't take any with me. I'm on my way to that funeral. As it is I'm somewhat late.

Oh, you're going there? Fine writer he was.

Yes, indeed. Good day.

He makes off down the Parade into the South Mall and crosses Parliament bridge to the South Chapel. Nice bird that librarian, he muses, have to try and find out her working hours. The priest, facing the congregation, was eulogizing. At the end of which, he said: "And now to close, I'll read a poem requested by the deceased:"

I must be off
I must away for
all around me's gone.
And one thing I don't want
to be the last man.
So off I must before
it's all too late,
better a bit too soon
than too late.

To those already gone, I
cannot bid farewell,
but farewell to you all
that's still around and well.

With my departure yours
is not far off, so
farewell again, for now
I must be off.

During the reading he noticed a certain disquiet in the congregation.

Then at last the "Ite missa est" was the sign to go.

Outside he heaved a deep breath, ridding his lungs of the foul air of candlewax, and prayed, not for the repose of the soul of the man they would soon be putting under the sod, but that the rain might hold off till the ceremony was over.

Chapter Two

Recalling the balladeer

They were sitting at a table in the hotel bar. Strangers you might say, just met accidently some few days before, and after a brief exchange of words, agreed on a date. The girl poured some soda into her gin, while he waited for his Guinness to settle.

Slàinte! He said at last, raising his: To poetry!

I'll be glad to drink to that, she smiled: To poetry!

It all happened so quickly almost as in a dream.

In fact, he was surprised she took the bait so quickly. During the few days that followed their meeting outside the Market, he wondered why she jumped to the offer. Apart from her hair, he didn't feel attracted to her, other than her interest in poetry. Was that all? And then, what were her reasons for agreeing? All speculating, of course, he told himself, and the sole purpose of their date had to do with his poems.

Well, what the heck, he said to himself, who knows what might come of it yet? Mary too was thinking along the same lines. I must have been daft, she mused, but let's see if he shows up. He too was wondering about their date, and was very happy when he spotted her standing outside the Met.

Hallo, he said, waiting long?

Just about a minute or two.

Oh, really, he said, holding open the door and ushering her into the lobby.

Lovely weather we're having, she said, it looks like summer is here to stay.

I hope so. To the left.

The girl was wearing a cotton dress with short sleeves.Her finger nails and toe nails were painted green. She had a small shoulder bag, and a Naomh Brid cross dangling from a silver chain round her neck.

When they entered the bar the bar-tender looked up and folded the newspaper that was spread out on the counter.

Hullo, he said, lovely evening.

You bet, Finbar said.

Mary glancing round the place, remarked:

I don't think I've ever been in here before, nice place.

Is that so? I drop in here from time to time.

Just days before, Finbar was standing outside the Market handing out flyers.

Like a poem? he asked, offering a flyer to the outstretched hand.

Yes, she said, I'll take one. Did you write them yourself?

Of course, I did.

Well, you're a bit of a poet then, she said, laughing.

I have a lot more at home, Finbar said,

Plucking up courage, how about tonight? We could go for a drink some place.

The redhead blushed. Sorry, no time till Saturday.

Oh, that will suit me fine.

It's a deal then?

After Finbar placed his glass back on the table, he pulled open the strings of his rucksack, and said: Talking about poetry, I have something here for you.

Mary took the notebook and began leafing through it, pausing from time to time while she read.

Have you published any of these? She enquired.

You joking? Nobody wants poetry.

But they're good, you know, she said.

Why, of course I know they're good, he stormed.

Do you often give away poems on the street?

Oh, gosh, no. This was the first time. It was one way of finding out what people thought about my poems.

And what did they think about them? She asked, laughing.

Well, there's yourself, for example, you seem to like them.

Mary laughed, still holding the notebook open.

Yes, she said, I find them good.

Loud voices from outside caused them to stop talking and turn their eyes to the door where a bunch of lads burst into the bar. They greeted the barman by name, and he in turn got down to business pulling pints of Guinness. The group remained standing at the bar with their drinks.

Finbar raised his glass. Slàinte! When he put the glass back on the table, he said to himself: Where was I now? Oh, yes, he thought, I'd like to explain to Mary that I was in the library last week, and looking through some poetry books, came across Raftery an File.

"Ag dul sìor ar m'aistear
le solas mo chroì
fann agus tuirseach
go deiradh mo shlì"

Going west on my journey/with the light of my heart/languid and tired/to the end of my way.

Finbar imagined the poet standing at a street corner and as Raftery put it himself, "playing music to empty pockets".

Mary looked at him. Raftery an File, she spouted.

Yes, he said, I was reading his poems recently, and I tried to imagine him standing at a street corner. I have never sent my poems to any publishing house. A few people I know, tried, but failed. So I ask myself, how are those blokes supposed to know more about my poems than I do? Bullshit! Anyway, one day I recalled that when I was a lad, there were the so-called balladeers. Those blokes used to go around singing in the streets outside pubs, and then they'd go in and try and sell a flyer of their songs. So I set about doing the same with my poems.

So, that's how it came about that we met outside the Market? Mary added.

Exactly.

As the evening advanced and outside daylight made way for the streetlamps, more people dribbbled into the pub. Finbar stood up, laid his rucksack on the chair and reaching for Mary's glass said: Same again? Mary nodded.

At the bar, some of the lads standing there made way for Finbar. He called his order and left for the Gents.

Well, what did people say about your poems? Mary asked, when Finbar returned with the drinks.

After sitting down again, he said:

I got no real feedback. Some few students stopped to enquire what I was up to. Of course they took some flyers, and wished me good luck. Then there was this smart Alek. Like a poem? I asked, offering him a flyer.

"What? Poems? What can I buy with them, young man? If you were handing out banknotes instead, you'd have a damn better chance of getting rid of them." Then he reached out his hand, "Well, I'll take one anyway."

Finbar watched Mary pouring Indian tonic into her gin.

Sláinte! He said, raising his glass.

Mary sipped her drink and said:

You remember Auden? "A poem doesn't have to be great in order to be good."

And how right the man was, Finbar added.

Mary smiled as she got to her feet.

Through the door, and out the back, Finbar said.

Straightening himself in his chair, Finbar glanced around the bar. Yes, indeed, he said to himself, Mary seems to be genuinely interested in my poems. She also seems to know a lot about poetry.

How she leafed through my notebook, pausing here and there to read, her smile sometimes glowing into a laugh. Very diversified, she mused, as if talking to herself.

You were saying, Finbar began, when Mary returned to her seat, you were saying, that a book, let's say a novel, once read, and put away for let's say a year or more, can awaken forgotten associations.

Mary brushed a wisp of hair out of her eyes. Let's put it this way, she said, you buy a book. Why? Somebody told you about it. You have already read some book of the author. Did you buy the book yourself, or was it a present? From whom? Once I was sitting on a bus next to a young girl.

Oh, The Picture of Dorian Gray, I said. Noticing the book on her lap.

"Oh" She made, turning and smiling at me.

"You know the book?

Sure, I said, read it long time ago.

Again Mary brushed a wisp of hair out of her eyes.

Yes, Finbar said, but with poetry it's quite another story.

Quite so, Mary agreed, here we're dealing with a story in a nutshell.

You said it, it's exactly that way. In fact, Mary, you just took the words out of my mouth. The beauty about a book of poems is, you do not have to read the whole book to get the story, you are free to choose any page you like. And in most cases the book offers you a variety of topics like sentiments, sensations, fantasies, reflections.

I notice, Finbar went on after a while, you seem to have more than a casual interest in poetry, would I be right?

Oh, yes, Mary smiled, it was my favourite subject at school. I find poetry enriches my life and fires fantasy. It's fascinating to see how the poet can depict such lovely scenes in such few words.

I had a very strange dream some weeks ago, Finbar said, it went something like:

Oh!...I think…well…now wait a minute. Think I know where we're getting…shadows deep…oh, yes…loved your grace...Ah, Yeats! "When you are old…" that's it!... and now go hide your dream in a cloud of sleep.

Finbar bent over and reached for his glass.

Isn't that weird, he said, dreaming stuff like that?

You're mad, Mary laughed, smacking him on the knee, simply insane.

You're right there, Mary, he said, laughing, s'pose I am. I always claim one has to be a little crazy to be able write a novel. But to write poetry, one has to be insane.

But this is a sort of sane insanity, Mary said.

Yes, Finbar agreed, there is supposed to be something like that indeed.

And this is what I call, Mary added, a benign intoxication during writing.

Wow! Finbar made, where did you get that from?

Well, Mary said, I'm sure there is a certain amount of madness involved.

Oh, very much so, I'd say.

Finbar got up. Think I'll need another drink to digest all that, he said.

When he returned with the drinks, Mary left for the Ladies. Finbar put his notebook back into his rucksack. Enough poetry for today, he mutters to himself, and see what the night brings.

Gosh, the air in here is putrid, Mary remarked, sitting down again.

Yearra, we'll be leaving here soon as we get our drinks, he said.

No hurry, Mary smiled, it was just a remark.

Maybe it's the gin, Finbar said, laughing. Mary grinned, maybe it is, she said.
Now, both sat with their drinks looking round the bar, as if the wind were taken out of their sails. The conversation around them sounded like the buzzing of an excited swarm of bees.

I suppose it's time to call it a day, Finbar suggested, taking his glass and emptying it.

We had an interesting evening, Mary said, as Finbar stood up and went to return the glasses and bottle to the counter.

Good night, he said to the barman, seeya.

"Thanks, sir, and good night."

On the way home Mary told Finbar she was studying literature, and that was why she was so interested in his poems. She'd like to work in a library.

People were walking about in and out of the shops. Others looked as if they were out for the night on their way to a pub-crawl, or maybe the flicks, or just going out dining. Suddenly Finbar stopped, fished a coin out of his trousers pocket and said: Heads, we go to your place, tails to me.

Oh, no, no, no! Mary protested, mass in the morning, and I must get my sleep.

Oh, Finbar made, somewhat forlorn, returning the coin to his pocket. And to break the rather awkward split-second silence said:

What would you say to a pizza, Mary? I'll have to go and get something to eat. Ever been to Italy?

I just ate before I came out, she said, I'm not hungry. And laughing, but you better run along and get something.

I think you're right, Mary, I'll do that.

And Italy, she said, again laughing, no I've never been there, you?

No, me too not.

They turned off Patrick street, and parting outside the Market, Finbar took her hand, warm like the summer night. He squeezed it gently, and said: good night Mary, till Saturday.

If that wasn't a kick in the ass, Finbar

thought, it was certainly a knee in the balls. Think I have enough of her, he muttered, on his way to Clancey's, where he called a pint and pub grub.

Chapter Three

…and if the letter is in Italian?

Collins avoided his local for a few days, during which time he spent frequenting other pubs where he spun yarns about some lost letter that some bloke found on the street. Now he was back at his local again, and had just called a pint, when a voice said:

Hallo Collins, where have you been these last few days?

Collins turned and looked at the man.

Nowhere in particular, he said, why, was I

missed?

The man didn't answer that, and reached for his glass.

Collins too brought his glass to his mouth.

So. Ye buried him, the man said after setting his glass on the bar.

We did indeed, Collins replied, if we're talking about the same bloke. Or have you per chance seen him about town?

The man burst out laughing.

Oh, Christ, no, he said, what I mean is, yourself was there, I suppose:

Collins knew the man but he couldn't put a name on him.

As a matter of fact, you're right, Collins said, I was very glad it wasn't raining. It's terrible to be standing over an open grave and it pissing down on you.

Oh, tis to be sure, the man said, a nasty place to be in any kind of weather.

That morning when I went to get the paper from the letter-box, I saw it must have been raining the best part of the night. But, luckily enough it cleared off before I left the house. However, to be on the safe side, I took along the brolly.

Bedad, you were right in doing so.
Collins emptied his glass.

So, I must be off, he said, walking towards the door.

A few days before, when Collins went home after the burial, he took the letter out of his pocket, and put it into the drawer of the kitchen table. We'll have to wait and see, he said to himself, we might somehow or other be able to find out something more about it. Macabre, Collins muttered, thinking about the poem in the chapel. But when you're gone, I suppose, it doesn't matter much to you. And yourself? He asked himself, pondering, have you chosen your eulogy? and laughed at the thoughts dancing around in his head as he sat down to write his article about the deceased and the burial for the morning paper.

"Passed away too soon", he heard mourners remark. But reading his works, Collins thought, one gets the impression, it's never too soon to die. That he was given a Christian burial was, for many of us who knew him, rather hard to swallow. His lyrics were not entirely what one would refer to as Christian. In fact, they expressed a great indifference to religion. On the other hand it seems all the more astonishing that he did not reject such a burial. Life isn't a reality. It's a pageant that we rehearse every day. You open your eyes in the morning and discover you're alive. Should you get up? Don the mask and enter the pageant? And that's exactly what you do. You have little choice, you're part of the cast. Folly, you conclude is the only word to explain life. A Fata Morgana that you wake up to every morning.

Before leaving the office the previous day, Collins said he didn't intend returning to the office after the funeral. Instead he'd write the article at home and send it by fax. Now however, it was still early afternoon, so he decided he'd go to the office. He pulled on his shoes and overcoat, and with the article in an envelope left the house.

Outside, as is often the case, the weather was better than he expected.

I didn't think I'd get away so early, he said, handing the article to the secretary.

"Thanks," she said, "big crowd there, I suppose. Did you get wet?"

No, he said, it was a bit of a wonder that it remained dry for the burial. But I had my brolly, he laughed.

"Doubt if that would be much use in an open graveyard" she said.

True, Collins said, but better than nothing, I suppose.

The phone rang, and the girl reached to take it.

I'll be off, Collins said, till tomorrow.

Out on the street, Collins got the feeling that he could eat something. All he had eaten since breakfast was a bag of chips after the funeral. He went into a fast food and ordered fried fish and potatoes, and coffee. The coffee tasted like… well, you know what I mean. And he thought about the savage flavour coffee at breakfast.

Tell me, said Collins, while the man waited for his Guinness to settle, did you ever find a letter on the street?

A letter on the street? the man repeated. No, he replied, I can't say I did. And what about yourself?

Me too not, Collins said. But a few days ago, I overheard a bloke telling someone about some lost letter.

The man looked at Collins, as he set his glass back on the counter. I suppose people lose things every day, he said, just read the Lost-Found pages in the newspaper.

You have a point there, Collins said, reaching for his glass.

Yearra, the man went on, that bloke was only spinning a yarn. Pulling a fellow's leg like.

Maybe you're right, Collins said laughing, it might have been something like that. But what I could catch of the story, Collins went on, was that the bloke found the letter on the street, saw that the house it was addressed to was just a few doors away, so he went to the house. There he discovered there was no letter-box for the name on the letter, so he stuck the letter into his pocket. The next morning he looked at the letter and saw that it was from Rome.

What? The man exclaimed, from Rome?

Yes, Collins said, from some bloke in Rome addressed to a woman in Cork.

But, tell me, what did that bloke do with the letter?

He kept it, of course, and considered what to do next.

And how did it all end? The man wanted to know.

Collins made no reply to that.

Here a kind of contemplative silence set in, which only after a short while was broken when the barman butted in.

The bloke in Rome will of course be expecting an answer to his letter everyday.

Well, Collins went on, I suppose hundreds of letters got lost every day. Don't you read sometimes in the newspapers how some postman dumped a bag of letters in some wood, or stored them in his flat for years, or, even in some cases burned the lot.

Yes, indeed, a man said, things like that happen. And then you have the case of letters turning up after 50 or a hundred years.

Quite so, piped the barman, you can often read about that. You ask yourself, where were they lying all those years?

Collins knocked down his drink. Well, he said, getting to his feet, it's something you can be talking about for a long time, but letters will continue to get lost.

The question of the relationship between Mary and Finbar was something fascinating for Collins. Could it be that Mary lived in Rome sometime? And what was Finbar doing there?

By now Collins had told the story of the letter so often, that he wasn't quite sure if it was indeed real or some kind of illusion. He was careful, however, not to mention a word about it at the office.

Downtown he would walk about looking at girls wondering if he could make out some girl that might have lived in Rome. I think we must conclude, he'd say to himself — here using the plural — I think we must conclude that Finbar was probably looking up some old papers when he came across Mary's address. So he decided to write her, never thinking for a moment that she might no longer be living at the same address.

Climbing the hill one evening after a short stay over at his local, he had just pushed the key in the lock, when a thought struck him like a thunderbolt. What, if the letter is in Italian?

After letting himself in, he hung up his coat and got into his sandals. Well, he said to himself, falling into a chair, if the word *amore* appears more often in the letter, then we must conclude — here again the plural — that it's a love-letter.

And if not…? Oh, man, what about your Latin?

Amo, amas, amat, he rattles off, getting to his feet and going to the bookshelf. Where is Longman? Nothing doing. He can't find the Latin grammar. He gets a sheet of paper, and sits down again.

Nauta puellam amat, he writes, how romantic!

Agricola terram arat. Collins laughs out loud. Now, he says, let us exchange the predicate.

Oh, Christ, I've done it! Cut! he shouts, not a word more!

Chapter Four

Off to Perugia

When I opened my eyes I immediately perceived some kind of humming or, I thought, was this a tinnitus attack? I got out of bed and went to the window while the humming got louder. I threw open the shutters and found I was looking out onto a piazza full of chattering people seated at tables outside cafés. Ah, I said to myself, no bees, no tinnitus. I glanced at my watch. Slept two hours, I said to myself. Well, I was tired after that long train journey, and then climbing up that hill in all that heat. I went for a shower.

When I arrived at the train station, I looked round to see if I could find a bus up to the town, only to be informed that during siesta the buses don't run. I had sent my luggage on ahead of me, so now all I had to carry was my rucksack. The signpost showing to the town centre pointed up a steep hill. Strangely enough, I thought, moving off in the direction of the signpost, there's nobody going my direction. Well, it didn't matter. It was a beautiful day, and I was glad to be able to stretch my legs after the long train ride. Still standing at the sign-post I looked up the hill like some mountain climber taking his bearings. Up there somewhere I told myself, shouldering my rucksack.

The train had long left the station on its journey down to Rome. The climb was easy enough at first, but the sun was killing, and gradually the way got steeper and steeper. But here I was now and there was no turning back.

"…and as I mounted up the hill, the music in my heart I bore, long after it was heard no more"

Ought I not have waited for the bus? I mused. Taken my time, gone for a drink at the station bar? Too late now. Wondering what she's doing now? I mused, my thoughts rambling back to my last date with Mary. No way, she said, pulling herself up on her chair, you know my position.

Well, yes, but wouldn't you consider it a good opportunity to take a break?

I have no interest in Italian, and it would require me giving up my job.

Finbar was in fact glad she didn't want to go with him, and after a short silence, as if deliberating with himself said:

I suppose you're right, Mary. And asked himself what would he be doing in Italy with a holy Mary like her?

The flyers, he laughed, and nothing came of them. "Playing music to empty pockets."

What do you mean, nothing came of them? She asked.

Oh, nothing, he said, apart from yourself, the feedback was very poor.

Oh, I see, she said.

Still no one interested in my poems, he said. No demanding I ought to get printed. No mention of me and the flyers outside the market.

Oh, poor Finbar, she moaned, you'll get published sometime, so keep on writing.

Maybe it might have been better if I stood there reciting my poems. What do you think?

There, he said, taking a letter from his rucksack: from the embassy.

Oh, so they answered you, Mary commented, taking the letter and glancing over it.

I've already made up my mind, it's Perugia, he said, taking the letter from Mary and returning it to his rucksack.

Their affair broke up before it really got started. For soon it became clear to Finbar that it was something of a platonic relationship. As it turned out, Mary was rather strict about her religion. So with their Saturday night dates and for Mary mass the next morning, anything related to fun was taboo. His holy Mary, it seemed had no interest in men. Her life was centred round her work, and as Finbar later discovered she had few friends. A pity, he thought, for Mary was a nice girl, and Finbar really enjoyed their conversations about literature. But what can you do? He asked himself, there is after all more to life than poetry.

So in the end he had no great problem leaving Mary behind when he decided to go to Perugia.

Will you write to me? She asked.

Of course I will. Hope the letter won't get lost.

Why? What do you mean get lost?

Well, letters get lost, don't they?

True. But nobody looks at it like that. Did a letter to you ever get lost? She asked.

Don't think so.

So you'll write then, she said.

Some weeks later when the new term of evening classes for Mary began, Finbar packed his bags and left for Perugia.

Finally the road branched off to the right and houses came into view. The climbing was over and the path now was level all the way. I had reached the outskirts of the town. The path lead into a cobblestoned narrow lane with houses flanking both sides. There was still no sign of life. Then, almost abruptly, emerging from the lane, I found myself in a corso which spread out to the left and right of me. This, I thought must be the town centre. My first impression was that I had just entered a huge cathedral through a side door. But there was a café not far away where a few people sat chatting. The tables were standing so far out on the street, that I was sure the corso must be a pedestrian zone. I stood looking round the place, and after a while went over to the café where I hoped to get a drink. The chief cook and bottle washer left his friends and came over to me. He wore a white apron reaching to his sneakers almost. And sure enough, just what the doctor ordered: Beer! I asked for a beer.

Bottle or alla spina?

Alla spina, I said.

"…for there's no good fellow when he's feeling mellow to the beer so yellow would say nay"

After serving me the beer, he lit a cigarette and glanced up and down the corso before taking a seat with his friends. While I sat slaking my thirst, I spotted a hotel sign a little way up the street. Again, exactly what I was looking for.

Chapter Five

Will Collins write a book?

The university is of course the central point of interest to the foreign student, and is probably the first public building he or she visits after arriving in Perugia. The palazzo is situated just outside the town wall in Piazza Galenga, so called because of the Galenga family that once occupied the building, and later donated it to the town to be used as a place of Italian studies for foreign students. The building is of Baroque style. Two huge wooden doors at the main entrance open into a hall with a very high ceiling. The hall itself is not spacious. There are offices on one side, and on the opposite side is the information office. A little further on the same side, after passing through a glass doorway, one finds the post office, where letters and cards arrive daily from all over the world. The café is at the end of the hall. Across from the information office a wide staircase leads up to the lecture halls and classrooms. The ceilings and walls of the smaller lecture halls are beautifully decorated with paintings of frescos, some of which are still in excellent condition. Amid such surroundings nurtured with trecento Italian and medieval history, the atmosphere of a by-gone age is ever present, and tends to bloat out the cosmopolitan reality of Coca-Cola, jeans and chewing gum.

Finbar went to the information office where he enquired about accommodation. The girl wrote a name and address on a slip of paper, and handed it to him. Then he went upstairs to check his registration. He had, of course, registered before coming to Perugia, so now he just wanted to see if everything was all right, and get his student ID-card. When he went back down the stairs, a man stopped him at the entrance, and asked if he was looking for a room. He said he wasn't, and went off to phone about the lodgings. The way into town leads through the huge Etruscan arch. The morning freshness was now ebbing, and the sun shone bright and hot just like the day before. Crossing the Piazza Novembre he walked down Via Calderini to the post office. Before phoning, he checked out the street of the lodging on the map he just bought at a newspaper stand. He found it was very central, just about ten minutes from the college.

When I left the hotel that morning and stepped into Corso Vannucci, I could no longer compere it to the quiet cathedral of the day before, life all over the place. People were now out and about. Some ambling slowly enjoying the morning freshness. People in and out of coffee houses others moved at a more determined pace, probably on their way to work. Some stood waiting at a newspaper stand while the owner was busy arranging the morning papers just delivered, in a wire display stand. Ecco! He said, and disappeared into his stand. A girl was washing down a shop window. She used a small ladder to get at the top. The hot water mingling with the cool air brought steam from the water in the bucket. The sun was still hiding behind the higher buildings. I went into a café and ordered a cappuccino and a cheese sandwich, which I ate standing at the bar.

A girl answered the phone, and said the padrona wasn't in. She would be back around 12 o'clock, so I could call around then.

Okay, I said, I'll be there.

I left the post office and went back to Corso Vannucci. There I encountered many students walking about, probably on their way to the college. Many of them spoke English; Americans no doubt.

I wandered off slowly in the direction of Via della Viola to see the room. When I got there and found the house, the door stood open, just like other houses that I just passed on my way here. I then looked and found the padrona's name on the letter-box. The hall was very dark, and when my eyes adjusted to the darkness, I made out a stone stairs leading to the upper floors. Although there was a window on every landing, it was difficult enough to see anything. When I got to the flat I pressed the bell. A girl opened the door.

Oh, yes, she said, when I introduced myself and told I had shortly before phoned about the room. The padrona wasn't back yet, so I would have to wait. But not for long as it turned out, for no sooner had I taken a seat in the small hall than the padrona arrived. A middle-aged woman, rather pleasant.

She greeted me after the girl explained to her that I had already phoned, and that she had told me to call at about midday. She carried her shopping into the back of the flat, and returned almost immediately.

"Yes," she said, she had one room vacant, opening the door in to a small room.

I thought, well, big enough for me. A bed, a chair, a small table and a closet. From the small window there was a beautiful view of the country-side.

"Over there on the hill is Assisi." She said.

I couldn't make out any town, so I called it the invisible town.

"No using the kitchen," she said.

After arranging the rent, I gave her a de-posit. I'd collect my luggage from the station in the afternoon, and pay her the rest. She gave me a key, and I left. I was now a resident of Perugia.

Weeks had passed since Collins found that mysterious letter, but he couldn't bring himself to get rid of it. Passing the address from time to time, he would stop and look to see if there was any letter-box for Mary. This fellow in Rome, he'd say to himself, pondering the matter, this bloke is surely expecting a letter every day, and nothing doing.

Could it be that my letter got lost?

Would he write her again? Or Mary might not be living there anymore. Maybe she got married.

The thought made him chuckle. Mary married. Mary in bed with a man.

"Nice bloke, Collins," someone would remark, "but I don't believe a word of what he's telling us about that letter."

"Having us on, you think?

"Of course!"

"Only a silly story," someone else added. "Maybe writing a book."

"Something like that, I suppose."

Gradually the topic became exhausted, and

it was only from time to time some bloke would say to Collins:

"Well, Collins, anything new about the letter?"

Divilabit, he'd reply, and say no more. At the bus stop one morning Collins overheard two men talking. Saying something about a letter and a letter-box.

"Maybe dead," the other bloke said. "Dead" the man repeated, looking at the other bloke.

"Yes, dead, maybe."

Just then the bus pulled in, and Collins missed the rest of the conversation.

Getting on the bus he thought, maybe dead. Mary Murphy dead, and a letter waiting for her in the drawer of my kitchen table. I'd better send it off to Rome and be rid of it.

Chapter Six

It's a bad storm that...

Murderous banging on his door in the middle of the night tore Finbar out of his sleep. Bewildered, he got out of bed and went to the door. As he did so, a blast of thunder ripped through the night. The girls stood there looking half terrified, and the padrona was calling on all the saints she knew, to have mercy on us. Finbar, realizing now what the fuss was all about, said: It's only a thunderstorm, 'twill be over by morning. Good night! One girl, Finbar didn't know her name, remained standing at the door. Good night, he said again, and closed the door.

He was just about two weeks in his new accommodation, when he discovered he was the only male in the flat. The women kept to themselves, though, of course they always exchanged greetings whenever they meet. They all knew English, but he didn't know what countries they came from. Fairly settled in now as he was, Finbar had found out where there was a laundry, a bakery and the bank.

Lectures began at eight in the morning, and went on till midday. Two or three times a week there were also classes in the afternoon from four o'clock. At midday most students went to the mensa which was just down a side street from the main building. The food was good. After the mensa he returned to his room to do some reading, or write a letter, and of course scribble down poems. Again in the evenings he often went to the mensa. From there he would go to some tavern with his friends, to drink Trebbiano and discuss all sorts of topics from language to literature to history and politics.

The first day of the new term, I went to the

university café for breakfast. After that I went up to the 1st floor to see what lecture hall I should go to. I found it on the 2nd floor. A large specious room with double rows of benches along the walls.

The professor's desk and chair were at the top of the room, and a blackboard hung on the wall behind them. I went and took a seat on the front bench on the far side of the room opposite the door. Many students had already taken their seats and were chatting with their neighbour. All eyes turned towards the door whenever anybody entered. But it was clear that nobody knew anybody else; all strangers from all over the world here to learn Italian.

The professor entered through a side door behind his desk. He was a tall middle-aged man wearing a suit and tie. He looked as if he were overworked, hadn't slept well. Maybe he drank too much vino, I thought. He put some papers on the desk, glanced round the room, and left again. He didn't close the door. The light was on in the room, and people could be heard speaking. Now there arose a sort of hustle and bustle among the students as new faces appeared at the door.

The professor returned, closed the door behind him, went and opened the entrance door, looked outside and closed the door. He stood at the head of the class, looked around at the new faces and smiled. Now we all stopped talking, and silence fell.

The professor went to his desk, picked up something like a microphone, and hung it round his neck. He spoke into the mike, but whatever he said, it was clear nobody understood anything. He went over to the benches and began talking to some of the students in the front row. Nobody understood. Then followed other questions. Nobody understood anything, and we all started laughing.

The professor kept walking around saying something to the one or the other, and offering the mike for an answer while we sat trying to make out what he was saying, and laughing at how some tried to answer in Italian. Then, after introducing himself to the class, he returned to his desk and opened a book that was lying there.

He looked at one of the pages for a few seconds, then turned and faced the class. He held a pen in one hand and the mike in the other.

"La penna," he said, holding up the pen for all to see. "La penna è gialla." And invited us to repeat what he was saying, which we did. And soon the whole class was answering like parrots.

When the lesson was over, the professor said "arrivederci" and waved his hand to us. This we all understood. And made for the door.

The morning after the storm Finbar got up as usual. If it hadn't been for all that hammering on his door, he thought, he'd probably have slept through it all. Outside on the wet streets it was cooler than other mornings, and the dark clouds moved rapidly across the sky. The storm was the talk of the place, also at the café where he went for a cappuccino and sandwich.

The storm, it must be said, didn't come suddenly. It was, in fact, expected every day, even hoped for. In the late afternoon, when the dark clouds would gather, eyes would turn towards the sky wondering if it mightn't rain that very night. Then, some hours later when the clouds dispersed, people would say: Well, there's no more chance of rain tonight, we'll have to wait till tomorrow.

The girl that remained at Finbar's door the

night before was the one he met the day he came about the room. Finbar didn't notice her at lectures, but he did see her from time to time standing in a group round a professor at some street corner. He was the professor for art. So from that he deducted she must be studying art.

At midday Finbar joined the other students on their way to the mensa. Waiting in the long queue, many were still talking about the storm the night before.

With his tray of food in his hands, he looked round for a table, and had just taken a seat with some friends, when the girl shows up at the table.

"Posso?" She said, placing her tray on the table.

Of course, Finbar said, prego.

"That was a storm," she began, sticking her fork into her pasta.

Well, if there wasn't all that hammering at my door, Finbar said, I'd probably have slept through the lot.

"You would?" she asked.

I'm sure I would, he went on. And by the way, sorry about last night, but after all it was only a thunderstorm.

You know English well, someone remarked, after the girl told us she was German.

"We should in fact be speaking Italian," she remarked.

"Oh, yes of course," someone said, "but we're having a break."

Everybody laughed.

"Ciao Silke!" A girl called passing our table.

This was exactly what Finbar was hoping for. So, Silke is her name.

When the other three at the table finished their meal, they excused themselves and left. So now Finbar was alone with Silke. But not for long.

However, now that he knew her name, it was easier to converse with her. Finbar motioned to the two Japanese that there was room at the table.

"I couldn't fall asleep after the storm," Silke said, after a while.

Really? I think I was asleep during the whole commotion, Finbar said laughing.

Silke smiled, and got dug into her tiramisù. Soon after that it was our turn to excuse ourselves as we got up and carried the trays to the kitchen hatch.

How do you like the flat? Finbar asked, leaving the mensa.

"Oh, it's quite okay."

Oh, by the way, my name is Finbar.

Silke, she said, offering her hand.

On their way from the mensa back to Piazza Galenga Finbar was assuming that Silke would take the direct way home with him. But when they got to the piazza, Silke said, she must go to the centre, she was meeting some others there.

Oh, in that case, I'll walk up with you, he said.

"This beautiful Etruscan arch," Silke said, as they passed under it, "formed part of the ancient town wall, and was a gateway to the town."

Oh yes, he said, I read about that. It was erected of these mighty blocks of stone, and stands an everlasting honor to the workmanship of that time.

They passed the café where Finbar sometimes went for a cappuccino in the mornings. The padrone spent some years in New York, so he knew well how the American students liked their coffee. The coffee was really good there.

By now they arrived at the beautiful Piazza Novembre in the centre of the town.

"It's quite a big square, and it is said, that when it was built it could accommodate the entire population of the town."

Here now, was the student of art talking, Finbar thought, and though he read all that himself, he let Silke talk away. And before parting at the fountain Finbar said:

And don't forget, we'll be there around eight o'clock.

"Okay," she said, moving off, "ciao!"

Back at the flat, Finbar found a letter for him on the small table in the hall. From Mary, he said to himself, letting himself into the room. He put the books on the table, kicked off his shoes and sat on the bed.

Hallo Finbar,

Thanks for your letter. It didn't get lost haha, but more about that further down. It seems you're settling in well. And how I envy you of the weather.

Hot and sunny, you write. But really Finbar, I couldn't have gone with you. How about the girls? Have you already hooked one of the olive skin sinorinas? And the beautiful view from your window of the invisible town as you call it.

How is your poetry doing? Any flyers being handed out? You remember when you told me you were leaving, and I asked you if you'd write to me, you said, sure, but there is no guarantee that the letter might arrive. Let's hope this letter won't get lost, Finbar. Write again soon.

Mary

Finbar stands up, folds the letter and puts it on the table. He looks out in the direction of the invisible town, and thinks about the lecture on saint Frances. Never heard it like that before, he says to himself. That was no wolf. No siree, that was a bloody whore.

The students looked a little stupefied. Had they rightly understood the professor?

A wolf? Makes sense though, he told himself, at least more sense than saint Frances talking to a wolf. The whore, it seems did in fact come to live in Gubbio. The villagers of the small mountain town were stunned when they heard about her. So it seems they went along to saint Frances and asked him for help. Saint Frances it seems didn't get rid of her, but instead, got her to give up her whoring, and she could remain in the town. Anyway, it appears that she agreed to his proposal.

Finbar laughed. Good story, he said out loud, still looking out of the window.

That evening Silke, as promised, turned up at the tavern. This repeated itself every evening, and soon Silke and Finbar became lovebirds. Their love-birding was always in Finbar's room, but Silke never stayed overnight.

Silke was from Frankfurt. She studied drawing and painting. She often considered going to Summer school in Italy, but dropped the idea, thinking it might be better to try and go there for, let's say a year. This, of course, meant she would have to put some money aside, in order to finance her stay there. Florence was, of course, her dream. But Positano was also a hangout for artists. Then someone told her about Perugia, so that settled it.

She started saving.

What Silke was doing in Frankfurt Finbar didn't know nor did he ask. On weekends the two would go off to visit Assisi, which wasn't far away. Or they took a bus to Lake Trasimeno. It was very enjoyable walking round the lake, or just lounge about in the sun. At the small snack bars you could eat fish and have a glass or two of Trebbiano.

As long as the weather was good, they used to travel to Ancona. This meant getting up earlier than usual in order to catch the first train. And though the mornings were light, the glow-worms sparkled on the bushes like diamonds.

From Perugia, which is perched high up on a hill, there is a beautiful view of the countryside down below. When fog gathers in the late afternoon, and you look out over the valley from *I Giardini* at the end of Corso Vannucci, you get the impression that you are looking out over a vast placid lake, with little islands or rocks sticking out of the water. These islands are in fact only little hilltops not yet covered in fog. It is not only a rare and picturesque scene, a scene fit for the Muses. It sometimes happens that visitors to the town arriving in the late afternoon, are surprised to discover that they are looking out onto a lake. This can't be Lake Trasimeno they think, and they never knew there was a lake so near Perugia. If nobody explained the matter, these same visitors were still more confused the next morning, when they strolled down to I Giardini to see the lake. And the lake? Where was it? No lake to be seen anywhere.

But the most vivid impression of fog and lake I ever got, was from a window on the top floor of the university. Looking out in the direction of Assisi, the fog covered the whole valley, and was just about level with the town. Here I got the impression of a huge lake stretching all the way from Perugia to Assisi, and the little lights of Assisi looked like houses along the bank of a lake.

Chapter Seven

Why not try Rome?

The lovely days of summer faded into autumn and, though the weather was still very good, the mornings were a bit nippy. Men had pulled on a jersey over their shirts, and the ladies swaggered up and down Corso Vannucci showing off their new autumn fashion. The term would soon be coming to a close, Finbar thought, on his way to the college, so he'd have to consider whether to enroll for the next term, or should he travel down to Rome in search of work?

At the café near the Etruscan monument Finbar ordered a cappuccino and a tuna sandwich, and went and sat down on the only chair vacant. After greeting the others, he said:

On my way here it just dawned on me that the term will be closing soon.

Most of the students were Americans studying Italian in order to study medicine at other universities in Italy. So it was no great surprise when they rattled off their plans.

Some would go to Pisa. Others to Bologna, some to Naples, and others to Rome.

All planed out. Finbar sipped his coffee, listening.

Well, he said, after swallowing down a piece of sandwich, it seems you have your plans settled.

Why? Somebody asked, what about yourself, any plans?

Ah, Finbar laughed, it was only this morning that I thought about it. The others looked at him while he drank down his coffee.

So what do you intend doing? One asked.

No idea yet, he said, but it's time to think about it.

Time to go, lads, someone said, getting up from the table. Finbar and the others followed suit, returned their cups and plates to the counter and wished the padrona un buon giorno.

Later that day Finbar thought, those Americans have everything settled. Should he consider staying on? He could, of course skip a term and see what's happening in Rome. And what about Silke? Had she any plans?

At the mensa Silke didn't show up. Well, nothing to be alarmed about; it happened from time to time.

When he left the mensa, he went back to his room. He threw the books on the table, and was just about to go and look for Silke, when there was a light knock , and Silke pushed open the door.

You're the very person I want, he greeted her.

Oh, she made, what's up?

Finbar didn't answer. Instead he took her in his arms and kissed her. Looking into his eyes with arms twined round his neck. Silke again asked:

What's up?

Finbar released himself from her embrace.

Tell me Silke, he said, what are your plans for the future? I mean when the term comes to a close?

Silke went and sat on the bed as she always did, and Finbar sat on the chair. She kicked off her sandals, pulled up her feet onto the bed, and leaned against the wall.

I was considering enrolling for the next term, she said, and you?

Finbar, feeling a smirk on his face, got up from his chair and looked out of the window so Silke mightn't notice his reaction. So, he thought, she has no one waiting for her back in Frankfurt. That was pretty clear. Just like himself and Mary. He wrote to her shortly after coming to Perugia, like he said he would. Mary wrote back. But then came Silke, and Finbar forgot everything about his holy Mary. He never wrote her after that, and neither did Mary write.

Finbar turned away from the window and looked at Silke, who sat holding her knees in her hands.

Why don't we skip a term? He began, we could go to Rome. We might even get work there, he added. You giving German lessons, for example. That wouldn't bring much, she said.

Well, maybe in a hotel, he suggested, pot walloping, he laughed.

Pot walloping? What's that?

Finbar laughed again: washing dishes.

Poor Orwell, "Down and out in Paris" or maybe I can get my poems published, and make some money that way, he joked.

Oh, great expectations, Silke laughed, but again, who knows?

Silke released her knees, placed her feet back on the tiles, and stood up. Never been to Rome, she said, going to the door, and you?

Finbar said nothing, and Silke just left the room without waiting for an answer.

In the bathroom she freshens up a little.

Rome, she said to herself, as she hurried along to her lecture, something to think about.

Meanwhile things had quietened down around Collins and his lost letter story. But he still had this letter in the drawer of the kitchen table gathering dust. What he overheard at the bus stop kept on repeating itself in his head. Maybe dead?

He thought about the burial he went to recently. Here today and gone tomorrow, as the saying goes. He turned to writing letters to the papers, and he himself answered his letters, using different names. No letter from or about Mary Murphy. Was the letter important? Not registered. That might explain something. Then the letter was probably just an how do oo do and how did oo did letter?

"O death where is thy beauty..."

Smart lad that Paul and his letters to the Corinthians. Wonder did any of his letters get lost? Paul, all the way from a fisherman to an eloquent theologian in a three years crash course. Difficult to imagine. But, there again the master was known to be able to perform miracles. Maybe that explains it. The devil, Collins exclaimed, immerging out of his reflections, I'll write a book about that yet.

Chapter Eight

The Spaghetti House

Life in Rome was very different from that of Perugia, provincial town, where as Rome was a sprawling metropolis.

Silke, who had spent some time in London learning English, declared, the only way to get to know a new city is to walk wherever possible.

We might wear out our shoes, she laughed, but that way we can get to know Rome.

So while they were getting settled in, they spent some time exploring the neighbourhood on foot.

When they arrived in Rome, they were very lucky to get a pension not far from the central station.

Back in Perugia while they were still considering going to Rome, Silke suggested they should enroll at the university. This would allow them access to the mensa, and far more important, they would have the chance of getting lodgings. But the very first thing Finbar did every morning was to get Il Messaggero. He had looked through it a few times in Perugia, so he knew it was the best paper to look for work. Most of the offers were for hotel staff or cafés, and Finbar knew there was no chance of getting work in any of those places without experience. But from time to time you could find an offer for office workers or even teaching. They had no set plans for exploring the city.

First to St. Peter's? No! After all we were not pilgrims come to Rome in the Holy Year hoping to do some good for our souls. Instead, we started off in search of the Colosseum. Besides, whatever can be holy about a year, a land, or for that matter, a person? I don't know.

The winters aren't cold in Rome. But, at times you can get a north wind blowing so cold in an otherwise azure sky, that you really have to button up. And this was just one of these days. And there it throned in the clear crisp light of winter, stanch as any Roman legion daring the foe to attack.

Just like you see it in postcards, I said, a monster of a building.

Indeed, Silke said, not taking her eyes off the building, what an impressive monument it is. Braving weather, storms and wars for almost two-thousand years.

Unbelievable! With such a building the Romans of that time must have considered themselves the gods.

No doubt they did too, Silke agreed.

Buses full of tourists pulled in at their parking sites, and shortly after cameras were clicking.

Well, Finbar we're not tourists, are we?

Of course not! It might even happen that passing the Colosseum might become second nature to us someday.

We'd better go and drink to that, Silke suggested, laughing.

Let's go then, I said.

We got jarred on gin, said Johnny to Jim.

With their new student tessera, Silke and Finbar could now eat at the mensa, so they had the cost of food fairly under control. Dining out was expensive in Rome. With the lodgings they hadn't the same luck. Rents were high and besides it was very difficult to find a place. When, after weeks of waiting they finally got a place, it turned out to be a two room furnished flat. No cooking facilities, and the bathroom was out on the landing. Well, better than nothing, Finbar remarked, looking round the place, I think we should take it and see how things work. They were glad, of course, for now they had a bit of privacy, and the fact that the place was furnished saved them having to buy some. And it was central enough too. Silke was glad she had a little more room for her painting materials.

At the college the information board they hadn't much to offer in the line of work, mostly au pair. Silke however had no interest in that kind of work. According to her she didn't get along well with children.

Like most mornings Silke and Finbar were having breakfast at the college café. Finbar took a seat while Silke went to get coffee and tuna sandwiches. When she returned, Finbar was looking through Il Messaggero.

Think I have something here, he said, looking up at Silke placing the tray on the table. Looking for English teachers, he said, must be native speakers.

Oh, she made, taking a seat, could be something for you, don't you think?

You bet, he chuckled. Know what, Silke, he said: I won't phone them. I have my papers here with me, so I'll get and see them right after I've eaten this.

Super, she said, and why not?

Finbar put the newspaper aside, and got dug into his breakfast.

I'm sure I have a good chance, he muttered, don't believe there are too many native speakers here in Rome.

Silke took the cup from her mouth, probably not, you certainly have a good chance.

Finbar was excited. Other mornings he'd go and get another cappuccino, but today not. Instead, after munching down his food he got up from the table, took the newspaper and his bag and said:

Wish me luck, Silke.

Oh, and the best of it, she laughed.
While Finbar made off for the door, Silke remained seated half praying that he'd get the job.

Two hours later Finbar returned with a bottle of Prosecco. He even managed to get a chilled bottle.

Got it! He crowed, throwing his arms around Silke, got it! Silke kissed him on the lips.

We'll have to drink this out of wine glasses, she said.

As you like it, he said, putting a tea towel over the bottle and loosening the cork.

To your new job, she said, as their glasses clinked.

Salute! he said. After putting his glass on the table he said:

Well, the only trouble is, it's part time, only three days a week.

Why, that's not so bad, is it? Silke remarked, better than nothing.

Yes, he said, there is a four week test period. The work is in the mornings including Saturday.

Well, having the afternoons free is also an advantage, don't you think so?

Very much, I'd say.

Well, now that you've work, I'd say it's high time I did something about my art studies, Silke said. So after searching for some time, she at last found a school of art not far from the Trevi Fountain. Classes were in the morning or in the late afternoon. Silke settled for the early classes, so she had the afternoons free.

That winter the cold spell continued for weeks. No rain and the cold sun shining in a blue sky. Nice enough weather, you'll agree, if you're well muffled up. But, at the same time, it's hard to stay out long in that kind of weather. What you miss is the pub. This sort of socializing isn't known here, and the scattered wine taverns seldom open before four or six o'clock in the afternoon. So you can either go home or maybe visit some museum.

But spring comes early in Rome, and the Romans welcome it with open arms, forgetting all the cold, happy again to be able to get out and enjoy life in the open. Dining at open- air restaurants, sitting around at open-air cafès or in parks.

More and more tourists flock to Rome, and waiters are busy collecting the tips left behind on the tables. And as spring rolls on and the weather gets better and better, people crowd to places like the Spanish steps, Trevi Fountain, not to mention Trastevere with entertainment round of the clock.

The vendors around Trevi and the adjacent streets pack up their merchandise, dismantle their stalls and close up shop, before taking a break of about one hour, probably for their evening meal. Then, when they're back again, they build up their stalls again, busy arranging their ware to attract tourists.

They offer all kinds of souvenirs, rosary beads, medals, pictures of the Pope. The year was a holy year, so there was, of course, great demand for everything connected with it, all selling like hotdogs.

Round about Trevi Fountain natives and tourists pour out of stuffy trattorie into the warm but refreshing evening air. Those who didn't take their espresso in the restaurant now stop at one of the bars to have one. Here everything is in full swing. People weave a friendly ciao to those they know as they look round for a seat at the fountain.

And then of course there were the groups of teenagers always getting the best seats at the bottom of the steps right in front of the fountain, where they spent the evening smoking and singing popular songs accompanied by guitars. Tourists groups stand around listening to guides telling them about the fountain. Later in the evening some old bloke or other would show up after a few wines and start singing. One of the favourites was "Quanta sei bella Roma in primavera…" *How lovely you are Rome in springtime.*

At last Silke got work in a German firm, which meant, of course, she had to reduce her studies at the school of art to two evenings a week. So, now that they had enough money coming in, they looked around for a flat of their own.

It was a semi furnished flat, which for the time being suited them well. But it badly needed painting. So Silke turned up a few days after they moved in, with a plastic bucket of paint and some brushes. It was enough to do the living-room and the hall.

Finbar often thought about their time in Perugia. His nice little room with a view of the invisible hillside town. It always brought a smile to his face. In order to avoid any trouble with the padrona or the other lodgers, Silke never stayed the night when they made love in Finbar's bed. So when his lad lost interest and dwindled, Silke got out of the bed and Finbar lay there watching her get dressed. Funnily enough, he thought, she was always without a bra, so she didn't have to harness her lollies. Then Finbar got up and kissed her good night.

Sometimes Silke and Finbar would arrange to meet at Trevi or some other place when Silke had finished her work. They would then go and have something to eat. The mensa was still very important, but now that they had a little more money to spend, they allowed themselves an exception from time to time. It was now late spring and the weather was getting really hot. One afternoon Finbar went to the Spanish steps where he even managed to get a seat. He opened his notebook and looked through what he had written over the last few days. Now that there was money coming in, he felt more relaxed, and that he could once more concentrate on writing poems.

After a while it got very hot sitting there, so he decided to leave and go over to Trevi where Silke and himself had arranged to meet. Sitting at

Trevi it was always amusing watching the coin fishers waiting with line and magnet to pounce on every coin the tourists dropped into the fountain. This was always a game of cat and mouse between them and the police. However, I don't think the police took it all too seriously. Often sitting on his own at Trevi the silhouette of Mary would creep into his thoughts. Did she get that job she was hoping for? Why not flyers in Piazza Navona? Hear ye, hear ye! Keep on scribbling, she said that time at the Met. "Nothing is but what is not."

Now he sat with his notebook listening to some fellow playing the guitar. Sometimes he sang French songs. A Frenchman, Finbar said to himself. Student, I suppose, but he plays well. After about half an hour he laid the guitar aside on the stone seat and pulled a packet of cigarettes out of his shirt pocket. Finbar stood up and went over to where he was sitting.

Hallo! Are you French?

Yes!

Are you studying here?

Yes, I'm at the conservatorium.

Oh, music?

Yes, in France I studied classic guitar, and

now I'm a year here in Rome.

He didn't know English well, so we spoke Italian. I told him I spent some time in Perugia, that I met a German girl there, and now we're living here.

It's hard to get lodgings here, he said.

Who are you telling? Silke, that's her name, and myself enrolled at the college, so we can eat at the mensa, and it also helps get lodgings.

The Frenchman crushed out his cigarette on the stone seat. Holding the butt in one hand he took a packet of fags out of his shirt pocket, drew one from the packet, offered it to me, which I refused, and pushed the butt into the packet. He lit up filling the air with the aroma of Gauloises. He didn't mention where he was from in France, nor did I ask. After taking a few pulls he took up the guitar and began playing again with the cigarette between his lips.

After a while he broke off playing, laid the guitar beside him on the stone seat, and took the fag from his mouth.

I gave a little clap of applause and a few others joined in.

The Frenchman smiled and bowed.

It's hot, I said, would you like to go for a drink?

Sure, he said, getting up and grabbing the guitar by the neck. I got to my feet too.

You probably know your way around here, I said, as we strolled away from the fountain.

Yes, he said, a good place.

Have they beer? I asked.

No beer.

What? I said, don't you think it's a bit too early in the afternoon for wine?

We'll drink Prosecco.

Oh, Prosecco, good idea.

By now we were entering a rather dilapidated looking premises. Well, I thought, he knows his way around here, I should think, so let's see. Inside it smelt of salami, wine and garlic, and looked just as dilapidated as outside. One wall was piled high with bottles of wine. Salami, cheese, hard boiled eggs, tinned fish and olives were on display on a counter. We passed a small room where natives sat at a table drinking wine. The innermost sanctuary was a very simple room with a low ceiling. Chairs were placed around wooden tables, and at the far end of the room there was a door to the kitchen.

Henri laid his guitar on a table, pulled out a chair and sat down. I took a seat opposite him. Henri called the waiter, a young man wearing a blue smack.

Have you chilled Prosecco? He asked.

Yes, sir, we have.

Good! Then bring us a bottle, please.

Minutes later the waiter returned with a bottle and two glasses. Henri opened the bottle and poured out the sparkling drink.

Salute! He said, raising his glass.

Salute!

This is on me you know I said. Salute!

Henri was a frequent visitor here, he told me. Although the place doesn't look much, the cuisine is good and abundant, and it's cheap on top of that. As a speciality, Henri recommended spaghetti agli e olio.

Must try it sometime, I said.

While we sat there chatting, my eyes wandered around the room, but nothing, only plain tables, plain walls, and the floor covered with sawdust. It was quiet in there with the only voices coming from the few people in the little room next door. Every now and then the waiter in the blue smack would fill a decanter from one of the barrels and take it into the little room.

During the hour or so that we sat there nobody came in. well, it was still early enough in the evening, and things didn't get underway here till about seven o'clock or later. Then there would be the usual crowd of workers from the shops and offices around.

As it turned out, Finbar and Henri became good friends, and often instead of going to the mensa in the evenings, he and Silke would go to Trevi to dine at the spaghetti house. Sometimes they would bring along some friends, and as often as not there might be a group of ten or more pour into the osteria. Then they would bring the tables together to form one long table where they all sat around. The young man would then lay aside his blue smack and don a white apron. Salads of fennel and radicchio, bread, olives and wine were served up while they waited for the pasta. The waiter would come out of the kitchen carrying a huge tray of steaming hot pasta, the aroma of garlic tickling your nose and bringing water to your mouth. Then one of the gang would get up and serve out the pasta to the waiting plates, and everyone got dug in. Later this was followed with pecorino, olive oil and pepper washed down with Trebbiano. When it finally came to paying the bill, we always left a generous mancia. Then we'd arrange back the tables and chairs as we got them, while the young man looked on.

Here is what Finbar wrote about the place when he first discovered it.

The spaghetti house

For want of a more precise term, let's just say it was a very simple eating house. This osteria was situated in one of the narrow streets around the famous Trevi Fountain. Its shabby outward appearance was in no way different from the shops, trattorie and cafés that kept it company. And if per chance or out of mere curiosity you stopped in front of its narrow doorway and glanced inside, well, what you would see, apart from the wall on one side piled high with bottles of wine, was not very inviting. However, it is far more likely that, unless you were introduced to the place by someone who knew the area well, you might pass it by for months or even years without even noticing it.

Sunday in Rome was the only day of the week that was quiet. But not so down at Porta Portese where every Sunday morning was a flea market. Natives and tourists flocked to visit the famous market. And despite the early hour there was as much hustle and bustle as at the open vegetable market at Campo dei Fiori. At Porta Portese everything was available from a needle to an anchor.

Many pensioners hoping to pep up their pension money offered things like cutlery, Delph, old clocks and watches, all sorts of tools, many of which were rusty as if they were just fished out of the Tiber that morning.

Silke and I were always amazed that so many people were there so early in the morning. But it seems that Porta Portese had some kind of hypnotic pull on people. With both of us now having work, we decided to remain on in Rome.

We no longer enrolled at the university, and Silke continued her evening classes at the art school. The following year after we met Henri he returned to France and we never heard from him afterwards.

Summers are hot in Rome and having spent most of our time scouting about getting to know the city, it was high time to venture outside.

One of our favourite places was to get a train to Frascati. The little town is the home to the famous white wines. The town is also well known for its villas and parks with their water cascades and terrace gardens. And so, as time went by in Rome – so lovely in spring – the Colosseum did in fact become second nature to Silke and me.

Chapter Nine

Cork lads in Rome

The scene that Finbar looked down on from high up on the Spanish Steps was nothing new to him. Mostly young people sitting in small groups chatting and looking through guide books. Every time he sauntered down the steps, taking good care not to trample on anybody, he thought about the first time Silke and himself came to Rome. However, today amongst the groups gathered there, he spotted a group holding small Irish flags in their hands.

Finbar chuckled remembering Silke's remark.

Isn't that the Irish flag down there in the piazza?

The Irish flag? I repeated, wondering what the green white and gold was doing in the centre of Rome. Could it be that the Gaelic League had opened an office here to bring the Irish language to the Romans? Or maybe it's the Gaelinn with their president a French man or Chinese without one word of Gaelige? Yeah, like a long time ago in Dublin with a man from over the water, if you get me.

That day Silke and Finbar were on their way to visit St. Peter's. When they got to the end of the steps and crossed the piazza into Via dei Condotti they saw flags from many other countries hanging outside the shops. The flags added an even more international flare to the atmosphere to the street with its many fine and expensive shops.

Crossing Ponte Cavour over the Tiber, though the sky was as blue as in summer there was a strong wind blowing, and the dead leaves scattered all over the bridge, were caught up in little whirlpools and carried high into the air.

A beggar was sitting on the bridge huddled in an old worn coat. He was holding a frying-pan in front of him.

Hurrying on through the busy streets and the cold wind they soon found themselves entering St. Peter's square with the great Dome.

This dome forms part of the wall surrounding the Vatican State. Nearly 90 acres of land fortified by a stout wall which cuts it off from Rome and the rest of the world.

The water rushing heavenwards from the two great fountains was being blown off course by the strong wind. Jarveys in one corner of the piazza, stood smoking to keep themselves warm while their horses munched something in their head bags.

Streams of children rushing in and out of the dome made it almost impossible for those outside to enter. Some of the children carried banners with numbers on them. Others held the names of their societies on high for everyone to read. All pilgrims from everywhere come to Rome for the Holy Year.

Where's the Porta Sancta? I asked.

No idea! I'm here too for the first time,

Silke said.

I thought it was near the Pietà.

Might be, she said.

Ah well, I said, might as well have a look round as we're here.

There were many masses being read in the small chapels on the aisles. Other priests were kept busy hearing the confessions of sinners from all over the world. It might be an interesting case for psychologists, I thought, to examine why people eat so many sweets while sightseeing in St. Peter's, and throw the wrappers onto the floor keeping the ushers continually on the go sweeping up the place. Little groups of people stood scattered about the building while a guide informed them about the holy place. Others sauntered about with guide books. Finbar was amused to see dust on the bare feet of some of the more important saints.

There! Silke said pointing, the Pietà.

It was enclosed in a glass case, and those standing around seemed to be looking at a wonder.

But where in the hell is the Porta Sancta?

Over there, she said, pointing. Over there

where the people are on their knees at the threshold praying and making the sign of the cross when they touch the door and the wall on the side where crosses were carved into the stonewall.

Well, if we didn't enter by it, so let's go out through it, I said.

One Sunday, years later Finbar was at the Spanish Step, and as he picked his way down the steps, taking care not to bump against any of those sitting on the steps, he spotted a group of lads with Irish flags.

Hallo lads! From Ireland?

All heads turned and looked up.

"Cork" came the answer in unison.

That so? Me too. Here for the Holy Year, I suppose.

"That's right. How about yourself?" one follow asked.

Oh, I'm living here.

"In Rome?"

Yes, in Rome.

"How come? Whatcha doing here?"

I'm a writer.

"A writer?" again in unison.

And now without further ado, they started

off saying something about a Cork writer that got some prize for his newly published book.

Sorry, I said, I can't say I know him. You see I'm living here a long time, and I have kind of lost contact with what's happening in Cork.

Finbar had taken a seat on the steps with the group. Now he rose to his feet.

Been to St. Peter's? he asked.

"Tomorrow."

Well, enjoy your stay, and good luck to ye.

So long, they said, same to you.

Finbar had lied of course, about being a writer. He had only published one book of poetry, and nothing more. White lie, he chuckled, moving away down the steps to the piazza. Could be indeed, he muttered, thinking about the writer. I wonder was that the bloke in Perugia? We mostly only knew the first names, very seldom the second name. Must look it up in my notebook.

Spring brought nice weather to Rome, so Finbar was at the Spanish Steps for the first time in weeks. It was then something of a coincidence that he met the lads. He was for a walk in Villa Borghese, and was on his way to the exhibition at the art school near Trevi, before returning home.

When Silke and Finbar got to know each other back in Perugia, they often spoke about their plans when they'd return home. Silke said when she'd get back to Frankfurt she was hoping to get a small atelier where she could store her paints, brushes, canvases etc. people could also come there if they were interested in her works.

Finbar told her about his interest in poetry, and about the flyers he handed out on the street.

Crazy idea, Silke said, laughing.

He spoke about Auden and what he said about poetry. "That a poem doesn't have to be great in order to be good."

You could extend this opinion to other writings, novels and so on. And, he went on, even to paintings.

Why can't you say a novel doesn't have to be great in order to be good?

Funny, he said, I always looked at paintings as brining colour into a room. Is it not something very special to be able to say, that a painting on my wall is a unicum?

A very satisfying feeling, don't you thing? How very nice it would be if people could see

paintings like this, Silke said.
Well, as things turned out, Silke did not return to Frankfurt, except, of course, to cancel her flat and have her belongings sent on to Rome.

Finbar, on the other hand it seems did not intend returning home. He had already cancelled his flat, and left some belongings with friends. His plans were to go to Perugia, and then on to Rome where he might get a job and hang about for a year or so. Then, when he'd return to Cork, he planned to take a course in Creative Writing. Later, when he and Silke decided to remain in Rome, he too took a short trip to Cork to clear up things and have his belongings sent to Rome. When he got settled in, he enrolled for a correspondence course in Creative Writing.

After completing her studies at the Art School, Silke joined up with two or three other Italian girls and rented an atelier.

At first she continued working, but as work at the gallery increased, she quit the job and took the plunge. She also gave German lessons.

A whiff of garlic greeted him when he opened the door to their flat.

Ah! He crowed, agli olio, my favourite dish.

Ciao Silke! He said, going into the kitchen, and planking a kiss on her cheek.

Oh, lovely, she said, I'll put them into water straightaway. Anything new?

Coming up later, Finbar said, I'll just go and wash my hands and change into my house attire.

Off you go then, she said, giving Finbar a claps on the bottom.

Silke went into the living-room and took down a vase from on top of the press. In the kitchen she poured water into the vase, chopped off the ends of the flowers and arranged them in it. She took the vase into the living room and put them on the table.

In ten minutes, she crowed, handing Finbar a chilled bottle of wine when he reappeared.

He carried the bottle into the living-room and found a corkscrew on the table. He poured two glasses, went back into the kitchen, and returned with two plates. He pulled out a chair and sat down.

Silke came in with a bowl of steaming hot spaghetti.

Wow! Finbar made, that smells good.

Buon appetito, she said, putting the bowl on the table. She served out the pasta, and sat down.

Finbar reached for the grated Parmigiano and sprinkled two teaspoonfuls over his pasta.

Buon appetito, he said, digging into his food.

Finbar was really hungry after being out so long, and didn't say one word till he finished his plate.

Ah! That was really delicious, Silke, and taking his glass said: salute!

Salute! Silke said, and took a sip from her glass.

Bravo! She said, a good wine.

Yes, indeed, Finbar said.

When Silke finished her plate, she got up and took the plates to the kitchen, while Finbar served a mixed salad in small plates. Silke returned with a pot of stewed fish, fennel and baked potatoes. After serving the food, she sat down again.

Well, like I was saying, Finbar began, his

knife and fork resting on the plate, as I was saying, I met this group of lads from Cork, over here for the Holy Year. And then I had to think about our first visit to Rome. Do you remember Silke, the Irish flag and then over at St. Peter's and the Porta Sancta?

Oh, Silke said, laughing, and the beggar on the bridge in all that cold? Did we give him anything?

Oh gosh, I have no idea, Finbar said, returning to his food. No idea.

And all the sweet wrappers on the floor, Silke added, laughing,

long time ago. Indeed, Finbar mused. As I had a little time to spare, I went along to the exhibition.

Oh, you did?

Nothing much happening. As usual, plenty of tourists about, but none of them seemed to have an interest in the exhibition; all too taken up with Trevi.

Well, I suppose that's how their guides prefer it to be, Silke remarked, don't you think so?

You're probably right there, Silke, he said, their whole object is to rush their groups from one sightseeing to the next as quickly as possible.

Yeah, I'd imagine it's like that all right. Both stopped talking and returned to their food. The fennel and potatoes were just right, al dente. Finbar mused thinking of how Silke's cooking became more and more Italian style. She had arranged a little garden on the window-sill in the kitchen where she grew basilicum, sage, rosemary and thyme in small flowerpots.

And what did you do with yourself? Finbar enquired, taking a piece of baguette and dipping it in the sauce.

Oh, first I did a bit of ironing. Then I sat down for a while with Fontamara, and after that I went about preparing cena.

Oh, Fontamara, Finbar said, it explains very well what the so-called high society thought about the peasants of that time, and how badly they were treated.

Yes,Silke said, Silone gives us a very clear picture of how the poor peasants had to fight for a drop of water for their tiny patches of land.

True, Finbar said, returning his glass to the table. Oh, and by the way, he said, auguri from Maria. She was all on her own guarding the fort.

What about Dario? Silke enquired, was he there?

Standing at the door, Finbar said, taking stock of the by-passers. "They also serve who only stand and wait."

Did he recognize you? Silke wanted to know.

Of course he did. Buon giorno professore.

To get back to the lads from Cork Silke, Finbar went on, I'm sure I know that writer they mentioned.

You think so?

Pretty sure.

Well, you can think about it, Silke said, getting up from the table and carrying the plates into the kitchen.

Finbar got up too and followed Silke with the rest of the ware. After Silke cleaned off the table, they did the wash-up together. After that they changed their clothes, and went out for an espresso.

The evening was mild, but instead of going on to their local, they decided to return home.

Once again Finbar changed back into his house attire. He went and took a bottle of Frascati from the fridge, and with two glasses went to the balcony, and put the lot on the small table. He pulled over a wicker-chair and sank into it. Leaning back in the chair and stretching out his legs, he thought about the lads from Cork.

Ah! Silke made taking a deep breath as she stood gazing out into the Roman evening.

What a beautiful evening, she exulted, spring in Rome. Then she dropped into a chair, and Finbar poured her a wine.

After sleeping late on Sunday, they went to visit the flea market at Porta Portese. Later, on their way home they went for a pizza. When they returned home, Finbar opened a bottle of wine. Silke took a sip of her wine, and settled down to reading her Fontamara.

Finbar got up and went to get a notebook. Over the years he had added a few more notebooks to the one he showed Mary in the Met bar. But it was just this notebook he took from the shelf.

His notebooks contained all sorts of information. Notes about poems, thoughts about novels he might write sometime. Sayings from books and newspapers. The notebooks also served as a diary when he was on holidays. He'd write about places

he visited, people he met. Sometimes he made little sketches of trees, the ruins of ancient temples, of a boat anchored in a calm lagoon.
He returned to his chair with the notebook and there between the pages he found Mary's letter. It was the letter she wrote him while he was in Perugia. My holy, he thought. She might be able to tell me something about the writer.

Finbar didn't say anything to Silke about Mary, and took the notebook back to the shelf. When he came out to the balcony again, Silke looked up. Find anything? She asked.

Nothing doing, he said.

Chapter Ten

Finbar considers writing to Mary

The next morning Finbar woke feeling a little jittery. He didn't sleep well, and every time he half woke, Mary was there.

Yes, he said to himself, getting out of the bed, he'd write a letter to Mary today.

Silke was up as usual, she insisted on making the breakfast. But she didn't seem to notice anything strange about Finbar, who was however glad when he was finally out of the house. Lessons began at nine and continued till one o'clock, with the usual short breaks, during which time he would have no chance of writing the letter. So when, finally the bell rang at one o'clock, and the pupils were gone out of the room, Finbar closed the door, went and sat down at his desk, and penned his letter.

The letter resembled more a business letter rather than a personal one. No time for sentimentality, he told himself, and added, besides, she might never get the letter.

Finbar put the letter into the envelope and sealed it. After writing the name and address, he wrote his own name on the back of the envelope, but he did not give his home address. Instead, he had the letter addressed to the post office. This way, he said to himself, there would be no danger that Silke might discover a letter from Mary.

That done, he got up from his desk and put the letter into the pocket of his jacket, took his bag and left the school.

At the post office he asked the clerk how long it would take.

"About two or three days," he replied.

Oh! Finbar made leaving the post office, making a quick mental calculation. Three days going, three days coming, let's say a good week and I should have a letter from Mary.

From Via Silvestro Finbar walked to the Trevi fountain. The weather was nice, in fact a little too warm for a jacket. At Trevi he went into The Spaghetti House and took a seat at one of the empty tables. The waiter greeted him, and asked where he had been all this time.

Oh, plenty of work, finbar replied, and to steer clear of any further explanations said:

I'll have agli olio, a small mixed salad and a glass of Trebbiano, please.

Finbar took a sip of his wine. Yes, he said to himself, we haven't been here in a while. Wonder where all the friends are gone?

"Boun appetito," the waiter said, putting the food on the table.

Thanks, Finbar said. The waiter went off and left him in peace, and he began tucking in. When he cleaned his plate, the waiter came and asked if he'd like another wine.

No, thanks, he said, I must be off now. Bring me the bill please. He paid and tipped the waiter.

"Hope we'll see you soon again," he said,

as Finbar was leaving.

Speriamo, Finbar said.

Outside Finbar glanced at his watch.

Silke isn't home yet, he said to himself, I'll go and sit down at the fountain for a while.

It was still siesta, so 'twas still quiet around the fountain. Somebody was strumming a guitar. Henri, Finbar thought, never a word from him since he returned to France. And then of course, Mary is probably married, he mused. Her husband opens the letter-box and finds a letter addressed to Mary Murphy, his wife's maiden name.

Lucky the postman knows her, he thinks, otherwise the letter would never have arrived. From Rome, he mutters, Finbar Barry.

Hmm, he moans, who's this fellow?

So you're back, Mary said, when her husband came in. What did the doctor say?

As healthy as a fish.

Oh, that's good news, Mary said, will I make you a cup of tea? What about your drinking, did he not say anything about it?

Not a word. And why would he too, he's no teetotaller himself. Ignoring her offer of making a cup of tea for him, her husband says:

Tell me, Mary, do you know anybody in Rome?

In Rome? Mary asks, giving her husband an inquisitive glance, while at the same time thinking, What's he up to?

Rome? She repeats. No, don't know anybody there.

No? her husband says, looking her in the eyes.

A nymphlike smile lights up her face.

Ah, now that I think about it, I do indeed know somebody there.

Ah, her husband trumpets, and who might the gentleman be?

The Pope, of course, she crowed laughing.

Oh, how awfully witty. Well, here is a letter for you from Rome, a Finbar Barry, does that ring a bell?

Mary takes the letter. Mary Murphy, she reads out loud, and laughing says, long time ago.

Mary tears open the envelope and glances quickly at the letter.

Well, fancy that, she sighs, Finbar living in Rome. What's this his name was, you said?

Barry.

Barry? I always thought he was called Barrett, or some name like that.

So you know him then?

And why shouldn't I? We used to live in the same street one time.

Oh, neighbours!

Precisely! He was always writing poems, and he'd recite them to us. I remember he told us he wanted to become a writer. At one time he said he was taking a course in Creative Writing. I'd know at the college or was it a correspondence course. That time I found it interesting, because I intended studying literature myself.

Soso, that's how it was. Her husband said after a while.

Of course, Mary didn't mention that she and Finbar were dating for a while. Nothing about their Saturday nights in the bar at the Met.

He came across my name looking through his notebook, she said after a while. He wants to know something about that writer that got that prize recently.

Ah, so that's why he wrote.

Mary put the letter on the table. I'll go and make

you that cup of tea now, she said, and scurried off into the kitchen.

While Finbar sat listening to the guitar, his ears captured the splashing of the water in the fountain.

"I will arise and go now, for always night and day I hear lake waters lapping with low sounds by the shore."

Ah, Yeats, he sighed.

Meanwhile three or four weeks had passed and no word from Mary.

Very fishy, he said to himself again today, just as he said to himself every time he left the post office.

Chapter Eleven

Collins must go to Rome

While Finbar was beginning to lose hope of any reply to his letter every time he went to the post office, Collins was still at a loss as to what he should do with the letter.

Two or three days after he found the letter, he said to himself, the best thing to do would be to go and drop it in at the GPO. But curious to find out what could be the relationship between Mary and Finbar, he decided to hold on to it. "Curiosity killed the cat, information made him fat." The thought made him laugh. And later, when this same thought got to really tickle his fancy, he began courting the idea of writing a book. Not that Collins had never before thought about writing a book. I *can* write, he'd tell himself, and add laughing, when I'm pensioned off. Maybe go off to some quiet corner of the world where the Muses are at home. A book about some lost letter, he'd muse, pondering over the matter. Bit abstract. And then, of course, what genre? Thriller? Romance? Crime?

If I'd open the letter, I'd know more about those two characters. But no. Fiction. All imagination. Maybe both were lovers in Cork sometime or other. Or could it be in Rome?

Finbar engaged in sorting out some papers comes across Mary's address. Long forgotten memories revisit his thoughts. But, could it be that this Finbar Barry wasn't a friend of Mary? Maybe just someone letting her know that her friend had passed away?

Here, Collins gets up from the sofa and goes to the fridge where he finds a bottle of Guinness. He takes an opener from the wall, a glass from the dresser, and returns to the sofa. He uncaps the bottle, and holding the glass a little tilted, pours the beer. He puts the glass and bottle on the table and waits for the beer to settle.

Pondering over what he had just thought about, he takes a sheet of paper from the table and writes the following.

Dear Mr. Barry,

I took the liberty of opening your letter addressed to my wife. It seems you and Mary were good friends a long time ago. Well, my dear sir, my poor Mary passed away last year, RIP.

He puts the paper on the table, and reaches for the glass. Well, he says, after half emptying the glass, and returning it to the table, that should do for today, don't you think so?

All sorts of suggestions kept popping up while Collins considered the plot. He imagined himself walking into his local with his just published book under his arm. Congratulations coming from all sides. Would he make it to a bestseller? he muses.

He looks around at the people in his local. No more talk about a lost letter, he thinks, not a word. And I here trying to write a book about it.

We probably won't find out anything about Mary, he thinks. But that bloke in Rome might be able to throw some light on the matter. Rome, he muses, if I want to guide my readers around Rome, I'll have to know something about it.

And what does Collins know about Rome? he asks himself. The answer is, devilabit. Well, of course, there is the Vatican. And the Colosseum. Well, yes. And then? Oh there was something about the seven hills of Rome, remember?

A short holiday in Rome, Collins heard himself say, what would you say to that? Not a bad idea. I would just need a few days to jot down the names of some streets, and maybe buildings. And then of course, we have Finbar Barry.

So a few days later Collins goes to a travel agent to enquire about a holiday in Rome.

"Great demand for Rome this year," the girl tells him, "Are you a pilgrim?"

Pilgrim?

"I mean with the Holy Year."

Oh, yes of course, Collins laughs, the Holy Year. Well, no, just a short holiday to get away from it all, as they say.

"Ah, well," the girl says, "I could fit you in in about a week or two. How about that?"

That will be quite ok, I'll get back to you then.

A week later with his ticket for Rome, Collins heads home delighted with himself.

First thing to do when I get to Rome, he tells himself, is to go and find this Barry, and have a bloody big bag of lies ready for him. Collins had fish and chips in town, so all he needs now is a Guinness, which he goes and gets from the fridge.

Sitting on the sofa he puts the ticket on the table, and beside it Finbar's address. All set for the journey, he says to himself, and reaches for his glass.

So, let's see now, he says, smacking his lips. When I'll arrive at… what's this the name of the airport…? Oh, Few me… something. I'll get into a taxi, show him the address, and off we go into Rome.

At Barry's place I'll press the bell. A male voice will say something, and I'll say: Hallo there, the name is Collins, I'm a friend of Mary Murphy. The voice will mutter something like oh, and the door will open. I'll pick up my allhold, and with the bag of lies in the pocket of my jacket, I'll climb the stairs. And just there on the first floor, I'll see a man with a mop of red hair standing. Hallo, he'll say, extending a hand.

Excuse my intruding like this, I'll say, just arrived from the airport. I'll take his hand, Collins, I'll say, pleased to meet you Mr. Barry.

Just inside the door of the flat, Barry points to a corner where I can leave my bag.

Can I offer you a drink? he asks.

Anything you have, I'll say.

Wine ok?

Fine, I answer, and add, when in Rome…

Oh, gosh, Barry laughs, haven't heard that in years. Mind if we sit on the balcony? He says, we have very nice weather.

Ok with me, I'll say, and fall into a chair. No sooner is Barry gone, than he returns with two glasses and a bottle of wine.

Cincin, he says handing me a glass.

Slàinte!

Barry takes a chair at the other side of the table.

Well, you were saying, Mr. Collins, you're a friend of Mary Murphy.

Yes, that's right, sir. Well, it so happened that I bumped into Mary in town a few weeks ago. In the course of our conversation, I mentioned that I'll be going to Rome in a few days.

Mary looked at me and her eyes began to sparkle.

Rome! she said, I have a good friend living there. In fact, I just received a letter from him some few weeks ago.

Is that so? I said.

Wait, she said, and takes a little notebook out of her handbag. Got something to write, Collins?

Course I have, taking a pen from my pocket.

There you are, Mary says, that's his address. Maybe you could call on him.

Should I take a letter or anything?

Oh, no, she says, I just sent off a letter a few days after I got his.

I see.

Did she say that? Barry will ask. She answered my letter a few days after receiving it?

So she said.

Funny, Barry mutters, I never got that letter.

Lost in transit, I'll say.

Looks like it, Barry agrees, lost in transit.

Well, I'll say, the best thing you could do now would be to drop her a line or two explaining that her letter never arrived, and you can mention that I called.

Is Mary married? He asks.

Oh, haven't the faintest idea. And I must admit, I don't even know where she's living. Mary and myself were at the College together.

Oh, he crows, no sharing beds or anything like that?

Not a bit, sir. Nothing of the kind.

Oh my God, Barry thinks, lucky Silke isn't here and all this talk about Mary.

With Mary and myself it was very different. We grew up in the same street.

Oh, he'll say, neighbours then!

Very much so.

I must admit, Barry goes on, I neglected writing her for some time past. And then a few weeks ago while looking through my notebook, I came across her address. So, I thought I must drop her a line sometime.

Well, I'll say, you wrote her, she answered your letter, but it never arrived.

Lost! Barry muttered, lost in transit.

I'll now notice the bag of lies on the table is empty.

Getting to his feet, Barry says: Well, Mr. Collins 'twas nice of you to call and bring me up to date on Mary.

I'll snatch the empty bag from the table, because I know it's Barry's turn for lies. And conducting me out to the door, he says. I would have liked very much to be able to show you a bit of Rome, but tomorrow morning I'm off to Perugia for a few days.

Barry offers me his hand. Good bye, Mr. Collins, I wish you a pleasant stay.

Could this be an opening for my novel, I'll muse.

Chapter Twelve

Too late, too late. R.I.P.

Collins opens the letter-box and finds a few letters. He cancelled the newspaper during his holiday, so there was no paper stuck in the box. He let himself into his house, and without even looking at the letters, throws them on the little table in the hall and goes for a pee. When he comes out of the bathroom, he throws off his shoes and slips into his sandals. Then he goes into the living-room, where he bends down and strikes a match to get the fire going. He goes into the kitchen, and gets a

bottle of Guinness from the fridge. He pours the beer into a glass, takes it into the living-room and puts it on the mantelpiece. After waiting a bit, he takes the glass, drinks and puts the glass back on the mantelpiece.
Pulling a chair up to the fire, he crows, níl aon tinteán mar do thinteán féin. There's no place like home, and sits watching the flames.

Passing his local on his way home from the airport, he intended dropping in for a drink. But he just couldn't do it. Back from a holiday in Rome, and they all wanting to know what it was like, and did he enjoy it?

Again he could feel his face turning pale at the thought of it. And he had planned everything so well. No, he told himself, I just couldn't tell them what happened.

After going through the customs, Collins went to the taxi-stand. He got into the front seat while the driver put his travel-bag into the booth. When the driver got in, Collins showed him the piece of paper with Finbar's address.

"Post office," the driver said, moving off.

Post office, Collins repeats to himself.

What the hell is he talking? Must have misunderstood him. Post office, he repeats again leaning back in his seat, around 30 km to Rome.

When they arrived in Via Silvestro, the taxi stopped outside the post office.

"There," the driver said, pointing to the building.

Bullshit, Collins thinks and pays.

The taxi moved away, and Collins was left on the pavement with his holdall. It was hot, nice weather.

Collins stopped a woman and showed her the piece of paper with the address.

"Is this fellow having me on? she thinks, "and the post office right in front of his nose:"

"Post office," she says, pointing across the street, "Post office."

Bullshit, Collins mutters, looking across to the building. Could Finbar be living over the post office? Better go and see, he thinks, taking his bag and crossing the street.

He enters the building and looks around. A sign on the wall catches his eye, and he looks at the piece of paper.

The sign read: Fermo in Posta, and under it was

written: Poste Restante.
Collins looks at the address on the back of the envelope and begins spelling out what was written there.

FERMOINPOSTA

Must be Italian for Poste Restante, he thinks. Collins swallows as his heart skips a beat, and he feels his face turn pale.
There was a clerk standing behind the counter, and behind him on the wall were rows of little pigeonholes with a letter of the alphabet under each one. More, Collins didn't notice. He must get out of here and get some fresh air.

Outside on the street again, Collins stands holding his bag, undecided as to what to do next. Gradually he feels life coming back to his cheeks. Anyway, I'm not going to find Finbar Barry here, he says to himself. And as he dwells on the thought, he mutters, bad start for my holiday. At that moment a taxi pulls up in front of him.

"Taxi?" the driver calls.

Yes, Collins says, throws his bag onto the back seat, and gets in in front. He pulls a piece of paper with the address of the hotel from his pocket and shows it to the driver.

"Via Nazionale," the driver reads, moving off.

In the living-room Collins sat gazing at the flames.

You bleddy rogue, Finbar, he says out loud, sending me on a wild-goose chase with your address in Rome. And I planning a gay time for both of us, having fun with some young nuns in Rome, as Crowley writes in one of his poems.

Hallo Mary,
I saw you doddor day.
You were chatting with that
Crowley lad
outside the Market gate.

In the living-room, Collins suddenly gets up from the fire and goes into the kitchen. You're hatching long enough in there, he shouts, taking the letter out of the draw, and using a knife, slits open the envelope. And now for the slaughter, he shouts, returning to the living-room, and sitting down again.

What a blasted holiday! He unfolds the letter and reads:

Finbar Barry
Fermo in Posta
Via Silvestro, Roma

Dear Mary,

I'm sure this will be a surprise for you. Well, you remember I went to Perugia. There I met a German girl, and at the end of the term, we decided to go to Rome, and we're still here. A few days ago I met a group of lads from Cork, over here for the Holy Year. And they spoke about some writer who won some book prize, if I knew him? Well, Mary, I couldn't say I did.

As it happened, a day or two later I was looking through my notebook, as I often do "in vacant or in pensive mood...", as some poet or other wrote, and I found a letter you sent to Perugia. The very girl, I thought, to throw light on the matter. So you might drop me a line in this regard. Hope you're keeping well.

Your friend, Finbar Barry

Collins tears up the letter into small pieces and delivers them to the flames.

Too late, Finbar, he mutters. Too late. R.I.P.

Epilogue

Mary Murphy was the girl Finbar was dating for a while before he left for Perugia. Mary studied literature, and after doing a postgraduate in Irish language and literature attending evening classes, she got the job she was hoping for, to work in a library.

Mary never married, and after her mother died, she gave up the family flat and moved to a smaller one.

The Cork writer the lads were telling Collins about on the Spanish Steps, died suddenly while the lads were still in Rome, and Collins was on his way to the funeral when he dropped into the library to return the books. The letter he had in his coat pocket was for the librarian at the desk: for Mary Murphy.

Mike Crowley

What Colette Didn't Know

Hans Konrad, department manager in an insurance company falls in love with a stewardess on a flight to Seoul. Later he discovers she's French living in Paris. She moves to Frankfurt, where they get married. Back from their honeymoon in Crete, Hans finds a letter on his desk, which turns out to be his dismissal. Hans keeps it a secret from Colette and goes out every morning as if going to work. Hans and Colette keep in touch by mobile, but on December, 6th on her way home from work, Colette wants to phone Hans, but finds her mobile doesn't work. She checks her notebook for the office number and dials from a telephone box.

ISBN: 978-1-911131-49-6

Mike Crowley

Pledged in Green

O'Leary arrives in Cork just in the neck of time to see his mother alive; two days later she dies. At the hospital he runs into Nuala O'Brien, a teenage girlfriend. This triggers off an affair which takes him to Cork more often than expected. Shortly before Halloween she invites O'Leary, saying she has a special treat in store for him.

ISBN: 978-1-907107-45-0

Mike Crowley

Wild Thoughts trapped in Verse

This little volume is a labyrinth of thoughts, reflections, fantasies, madness. Ever present is the author's devilish companionship with the Muses. Thoughts, fly around like satellites speeding through space, are harnessed to complete the jigsaw puzzle. Chaos becomes woven into verse.

ISBN: 978-1-911131-57-1